**Most people will get distracted
by the
garbage of life!**

Will you be one of them?
OR
Will you discover...

The Secret of the Can

First Edition
Copyright © 2008 by Larry Tracey

Larry Tracey
PO Box 108
North Olmsted, OH 44070
USA

Edited By Sue Starr

ISBN: 978-0-9802232-1-7

Dedication

Lawrence J. Tracey, Sr. (1926 – 1951)

Dedicated to all the members of

Youth4Youth

Past, Present and Future

Dedicated to all those who have been

distracted by the garbage of life;

may you discover how to

"let go" and follow your dreams!

Gratitude

Many have encouraged me to write this book…friends and people I did not know but who heard my message when I would speak at their school or organization. We each have people like this in our lives. I encourage you to take the opportunity to think of who they are and send them a thought of love and gratitude.

Mom, Dad, and Og Mandino
You were the inspiration for the work I do with youth, educators, and parents.

Joe, Brian, and Dan
You gave me the privilege to be your father.

Jack Canfield
Your love and support as teacher, mentor and friend.

The Platinum Mastermind Alliance
For your love and support past, present and future.

Jim Bunch
This book is a result of our laser coaching session.

Judy Grabowski
It takes a special person to see the bigger vision for change and making a difference in the world.
Thank you for pushing me to stay focused.

The Secret of the Can

Contents

Introduction

Many people will enter our life, through a song, a book, a dream and more. From them, we unknowingly receive insight, guidance and answers. As quickly as some enter…they will disappear. When you become **aware** of this possibility you become **open** to all the opportunities in life. The sad part is, many will miss life's opportunities, as they get *"distracted by the garbage of life."*

As for myself, I spent many years blind to opportunity because I was preoccupied by the garbage and drama of life. As a senior in high school my perception of myself was that I was dumb and stupid, I wasn't getting it…but everyone around me in class was. I would read and it wouldn't make sense, it would mean the opposite or I couldn't focus on the words. I got tired and wanted to fall asleep…I wanted nothing to do with reading. I quit reading for 13 years.

Thirteen years later, life had progressed or should I say regressed, to where I needed a miracle to occur. I was at a yard sale and I picked up a thin paperback book written by a man named Og Mandino. I felt someone walk up beside me. I glanced to my left and saw an older lady. She smiled, touched my arm and softly said, "Sir, I want you to have that book." I offered to pay her but she refused. She made me promise I would read it and I agreed.

That was my starting point of *awareness*. As I tell many of the groups I speak to, "Most people can look back to one instance in their life where the words of another have made the difference. Someone made that same difference in me; back in 1984...I'm very grateful for the opportunity to return the favor.

Chapter

Illusions

"Everything is an illusion, so pick one that's empowering."

- Christine Comaford-Lynch

Hey, I'm Reese Williams and I'm a junior in high school. Adults tell me I have something called "potential." I have it. You have it. Everyone has it. But the garbage of life, you know, the stuff that distracts most people, never allows them to reach their full *potential* and explore all life's possibilities. And you know what the sad part is? Most people will actually accept and believe those distractions…those illusions.

Welcome to my life…my internal thoughts and judgments.

January 20 – Journal Entry

Part of our Life Skills class is journaling and it's 50% of our grade. In the beginning I remember thinking this is so unfair…50% of my grade…gimme a break…only girls do this stuff. This totally sucked. There must be a law against this. What does this have to do with Life Skills anyhow? How could my teacher do this to me?

But you know what? Writing has become a habit. I can express myself better and journaling has actually helped me get clear on my goals, discover answers to problems and I get in less trouble because I don't take my feelings out on others. The best part is I don't have to hold onto any old or bad feelings anymore. I can let them go by writing them down. Many times after I write about things that I thought were a big deal, really aren't that important anymore.

So here I am entering the second half of my junior year in high school …it's second period and I'm in Tibbit's math class right now and I'm journaling. Am I insane or what? Get a life! Anyhow, back to Tibbit's and math…I sure am glad I have him in the morning. If it were in the afternoon he would put me to sleep. This math stuff…well, I think I know it – but when it comes to the test, I work out the answer and its usually wrong. I used to think I was good in math but lately…

Reading…that's another story…I don't understand what I read most of the time. It's like it doesn't even begin to sink in. I have a hard time following ideas and I'll read something and get the opposite of what it's supposed to mean. So I read as little as possible, cheat if I can, but then I end up feeling guilty inside. One of our English projects last month was to do a survey with the whole school and we discovered that only 20% of the students like to read. I wonder why that is? My mom and grandma tell me reading is the most important thing I will learn – but really….what do *they* know?

Met a girl named Suzie last Friday. She's hot. Can't get her off my mind. Why can't I ever have a hot teacher? I bet then I would learn…my Life Skills teacher, well she was hot and look…here I am journaling. I said, "*Was* hot" because she just had a baby girl and is on maternity leave. We're supposed to have a substitute teacher starting this semester who's name is Mr. Austin Walker.

Since this is the first day of the second semester every teacher will be going over the class rules. I have six classes which means I have to remember six different sets of rules and procedures…yada, yada, yada.

January 21 – Journal Entry

In Civics now and should be paying attention but you want to know the truth? I think my civics teacher was stuck teaching this subject because they didn't know what else to do with him. I'm not sure if he did something wrong and this is his punishment or if they are punishing us.

This stuff makes no sense and what good would it do me anyway? I bet this guy got straight A's in Boring. How does someone get to be such a boring teacher? That must be a college class you have to take to become a teacher...Boring 101. I bet you have to take four years of it to be a teacher. There's Boring 101, followed by Boring 102…

People think I have it all together but they really don't know what goes on inside me, or do they? Inside I have my own ideas of what people are thinking of me and I'm beginning to see they are...*judgments of myself*. Many are **other** people's words, opinions, and judgments about me that I have started to believe. Some are good and some are bad. When I really look at those ideas, they are really my own judgments about myself that I believe to be true. I guess I should decide who I am and who I'm going to be and avoid blaming others. Otherwise, I could spend a good part of my life in self-doubt and criticism, which would really hold me back or just flat-out suck. My guess is that we all walk around thinking about what others are thinking about us, when in reality they are wondering what I am thinking about them. Wow! I bet people waste a lot of time doing that. I'd better not think too much about this. I could get lost in my thoughts and never be found again.

People, life and the way we treat each other is sometimes so confusing to me. We all judge others and ourselves. There's all this drama, distraction and garbage. People seem to thrive on this stuff. The halls were buzzing this morning. I mean literally, you could hear it everywhere. There was this party on Saturday night and a couple of students were in a bedroom, someone came in pulled off the covers and took a picture and then text messaged it to a bunch of people. Everyone was looking at it and with the speed this thing was spreading it will only be a matter of time before someone gets in some serious trouble. I can't believe the girl came to school today. She has become the center of attention to say the least. One poor choice and your life can change forever.

There seems to be all this intensity and energy around ruining others' lives and the negativity that comes with it...it's like an addiction. People get bored, create drama and that creates intensity. I wonder if you can be positive and create the same effect? Wow Reese, there's a thought to hang on to...I think you should try that in the future. Mr. Walker, our Life Skills substitute teacher, threw us a curve yesterday...he says we have no rules, only guidelines. He obviously hasn't been a teacher before.

January 22 - Journal Entry

A lot of buzz in the halls again today; those text pictures are all over the internet now. But the real buzz is the girl tried to commit suicide by taking a bunch of pills. She passed out in second period class and they called 911. No one is sure if she's okay...I mean alive. Everyone knows about it now.

Mr. Walker – I'm not sure about him. He's different somehow...but I can't put it into words yet. My friend Delaney Foster said, "He is a *person of substance*...yet it's like he's not really there." Now you have to understand Delaney, she is out there sometimes with her thinking. Exactly what is a *person of substance* and how can you have substance but not really be there? But that's Delaney! She's plain and doesn't stand out – just an average student. She's involved in drama club and really comes alive when she's on stage. That *'person of substance'* stuff probably was a line in a play she's quoting.

She's been raised by her dad cause her mom left when she was three. I've heard children need one close adult in their life to be successful, someone they can trust and confide in and it doesn't have to be a parent. I bet it would help if more kids knew that. She has that in her dad and having that one person makes all the difference. I wish my mom and I were close. She has to work a lot just to make ends meet.

There are many times when I feel so alone.

As for myself, I never had a father. I'm not doing as well as I could in school and I tend to do enough just to get by. I'm involved in basketball and track so that motivates me to stay eligible for the team. Mom seems frustrated with my grades and me and it seems like she's always on my back about something. She worries too much. I wish she would stop being so overprotective and leave me alone. Maybe she finally is…yah!

I tend to get distracted easily and see myself as unorganized. Delaney says I have A.D.D.. I love to draw and many times find myself drawing during class time when I should be paying attention. There is one particular drawing I always make. Actually, I've gotten pretty good with it and can do the whole thing in less than a minute. It's this old man and his leather pouch.

Speaking of A.D.D., I was writing about our substitute teacher and the next thing you know I'm writing about my artistic ability. Oh yes, Mr. Walker, there's something about him…no drama…no pressure, relaxed and… I feel like I have known him a long time…yet we've just met.

January 23 – Journal Entry

This is a strange situation – a substitute teacher – Mr. Walker – has no rules just guidelines but has complete control of the whole class, yet he is not controlling. As a class we had a discussion about respect and responsibility and now when I enter this room something happens, it seems like there's an expectation, an attitude. It's like there is this unwritten agreement. I feel I'm responsible for everything that happens to me. I am in control, yet he is in control without being controlling. This is so confusing. Here is a classroom that looks like any other classroom...but it feels different. Something happens when you walk through the door. It feels strange – different. I can't explain it but it actually feels good. Now I'm beginning to sound like Delaney. Delaney lookout – you've got competition!

"The greatest discovery of my generation is that a man can alter his life simply by altering his attitude of mind."

– William James

January 24 – Classroom Experience

It's the end of our first week with Mr. Walker and I'm beginning to understand his style. One word to describe it – different! Life Skills is the last period of the day so

every one is anxious to leave, especially because it's
Friday.

"I believe you are all straight 'A' students," Mr. W
said!

Eric piped up and said, "I've never gotten an 'A' in my
life, why start now?" Sally and Sam are both straight "A"
students so you could see their excitement and confidence
... as they waved their hands like they were bragging.

Mr. Walker continued, "Today is our first test." You
could hear a big moan come from the class.

Jessie shouted, "This is soooo unfair. Our first week, a
surprise test and you think we're all straight 'A'
students?" Everyone laughed.

"You didn't even tell us what to study," said Jake.

Mr. Walker calmly smiled and continued on. He wrote
the following on the Smartboard:

What parts of life are you getting A's in?

He passed out the test and we had to give ourselves a
letter grade in the following areas:

____ Being on time for school
____ Being on time for class
____ Writing down my assignments
____ Doing homework
____ Taking notes in class
____ Studying
____ Asking questions in class
____ Keeping an organized locker

____ Bath or shower each day
____ Keeping a clean bedroom
____ Brush teeth two or more times daily
____ Obeying parents
____ Telling the truth
____ Treating teachers with respect
____ Not making fun of others
____ Keeping my commitments
____ Not being a bystander when someone is bullied
____ Not spreading rumors about others
____ Good listener
____ Show appreciation
____ Helping others
____ Driving the speed limit
____ Having a positive role model in my life
____ Have two or more close friends
____ I do not use profanity
____ I give 100% at my job
____ I have one or more supportive adults in my life
____ I do not steal from my employer
____ I give 100% in schoolwork
____ I give 100% in team sports
____ I do not engage in drug use
____ I do not engage in alcohol use
____ I do not engage in sexual activity
____ I do not engage in nicotine use
____ I am a leader
____ I believe in myself
____ Good friend
____ Can I be trusted?
____ Can others always count on me?
____ I compliment others
____ Involvement in extracurricular school activities
____ Taking responsibility for everything that happens
     to me

When everyone finished, Mr. Walker once again said, "I believe you are all straight 'A' students. Many of you just don't see yourself that way. You get an "A" in every choice you make regardless of the outcome. Do I have a volunteer to help the class understand this?"

Eric raised his hand. "Eric, what did you give yourself in locker organization?"

"F," he said proudly.

"But if you graded yourself for having a messy locker what grade would you give yourself?"

"An 'A' sir," he replied.

"You are an 'A' student Eric because you choose to keep a messy locker. Eric, how is your 'A' in messy locker working for you?"

"It works pretty good," Eric joked. Delaney and Sam LOL.

Sam shared, "Yah right, you're always borrowing my book and yesterday you told Tibbits."

Mr. Walker interrupted, "Mr. Tibbits."

"Sorry sir. You told Mr. Tibbits, you knew you did the assignment but couldn't find it," said Sam.

"Is that correct Eric?" Mr. Walker asked.

"Well, yes sir," replied Eric.

"No well about it. Either yes or no."

"Yes sir," said Eric as he looked down at his desk.

"Busted," someone shouted.

Mr. Walker continued. "Has getting an 'A' in messy locker caused lower grades in other areas…by being late to class or not being able to find your book to take home to complete a homework assignment because looking would cause you to miss your bus?"

"Yes sir," Eric responded.

"So how is that behavior working for you?" asked Mr. Walker.

"It's not sir."

"Would you like to change that behavior Eric?"

"Well maybe," said Eric.

"Chad you had your hand up. Chad, in doing your homework you gave yourself a "D" because you really never do homework. But what if you graded yourself on not doing homework?" asked Mr. W.

"I'd get an A, no questions," said Chad.

Mr. Walker smiled and said, "So Chad, you too are an 'A' student. How is getting 'A's in not doing your homework working for you?"

Chad responded, "I guess I'm cornered on this one. I can't make excuses can I Mr. W?

"That's a very good point Chad," Mr. Walker cut in, "When you take responsibility for everything that happens to you, you no longer make excuses. You get to the truth faster."

Chad continued, "Well, the truth is Mr. W, if I did my homework I would probably have at least a 'B' average in all my classes."

"Chad, do you think doing homework would help you remember more information on your tests?"

"I guess so...I mean, yes it would," Chad confidently responded.

"Then you probably could be an 'A' student by changing just one behavior," Mr. W added.

"Yah, I never saw it that way. Thanks!" cheered Chad.

Mr. Walker then asked in an inquisitive voice, "I'm curious how everyone answered these two questions...but I want you to do this in the silence of your own mind."

1. **What grade would you get in making fun of other people?**

2. **What grade would you get in spreading rumors and gossip about others?**

After a minute Mr. Walker asked us to give ourselves a letter grade on the entire test keeping in mind there were no right or wrong answers. The only thing that counted was our honesty.

Next he had us pick the two behaviors we could change that would have the biggest impact on our life. Write them on the back of our paper, share them with someone else and then hand the paper in.

The bell rang and everyone left joking about their "A's" in life.

Reese was the last to leave the room. Mr. Walker said, "Reese, I noticed you didn't raise your hand, but yet your face showed there was a lot going on inside of you. Is that true?"

"Well sir, I kept my hand down because I didn't want to be embarrassed by answering questions and then be made fun of and laughed at by everyone else. Excuse me for saying sir, but you cut through all the crap and got right to the point. You're like a laser beam," shared Reese.

"Thank you Reese," Mr. Walker said with a big smile. "I'll take that as a compliment. Life is too short and people waste so much time because they are unable to be honest with themselves. I've found if you make a few positive changes in life, as a teen, then that will make all the difference in the end. But something tells me there's much more going on inside of you Reese."

Reese broke eye contact with Walker and said, "Well Mr. W, I've got to go, we have a big game tonight against Southwest and I'm changing my behavior of "being late" so I've got to run. See you on Monday!"

"Good luck tonight and sink a three for me!" Walker added.

January 26 – Journal Entry

I've been thinking about my conversation with Mr. Walker after class on Friday. How does he know there is stuff going on inside me? Is it that obvious? Sometimes I feel like I get lost in my own mind and the feelings of the past…pain, jealousy, anger, and loneliness.

I become silent and withdrawn at times. Sunday nights are especially lonely for me. I wonder why?

My bright spot – We won Friday night's game against Southwest 61-58. I was 3 of 4 in three-point shots and ended the game with 11 points. I even thought of Mr. W when I made my last 3-pointer! Oh yah, I wonder why Mr. W wears that leather pouch on his belt?

Chapter 2

No Protection

"Pain is inevitable. Suffering is optional."

– Anon.

January 27 – Class Experience

We began today with a journal entry in Life Skills. Everyone had to write about a defining moment in his or her life, an event that *changed* his or her life.

January 27- Journal Entry

My first father died eight months before I was born. While other kids had a father, I didn't. I wasn't able to play football because my mom was worried I'd get hurt. All the cool kids played football and I felt left out. My mom was overprotective. I felt like I didn't fit in although I wanted to really bad. So being alone was good. No one to put you down, make fun of you, or make you feel inferior. Was I too sensitive? I would take the opinions and comments of other people too personally. Other kids seemed mean and ruthless. Most of the time I felt I was the odd man out. I would feel inferior, less than, and stupid. I seemed to always be fighting for my survival. I really don't want to write anymore because those feelings of pain and loneliness are coming up again. I bet Mr. Walker is going to ask a few of us to share and help the class. Don't know if I'm that brave.

Mr. Walker asked for sharing but we were only supposed to share the event. Delaney raised her hand. "I'll go. My mom left when I was three and I haven't seen her since."

"My neighbor's house burnt down when I was four," shared Sara, "It was the middle of the night and I still feel scared when I think about it."

Jason shared, "When I was five my parents got divorced and my mom and I moved here."

Reese raised his hand and Mr. Walker nodded. "My dad died eight months before I was born, so I never met him."

"I was called 'Miss Piggy' in elementary school and my mom would say I'm going to be fat," Amanda shared softly.

Mr. Walker asked, "Would you all agree that everyone has experienced moments that have affected them?" The class nodded in agreement. **"From our defining moments we make decisions about life and those become our beliefs and our beliefs become our reality. As we grow older we hold onto those beliefs even though they may no longer apply. So if we want to change our reality we have to change our beliefs."**

Just then, the bell rang and the class left quietly.

"Even though you may want to move forward in your life, you may have one foot on the brake. In order to be free, we must learn how to let go. Release the hurt. Release the fear. Refuse to entertain your old pain. The energy it takes to hang onto the past is holding you back from a new life. What is it you would let go of today?"

- Mary Manin Morrissey

January 28 – Class Experience

I noticed everyone left quietly after yesterday's class. "What were your thoughts?" asked Mr. Walker.

Reese raised his hand. "Mr. W, it seems like kids have no way of protecting themselves from things."

"Very good observation Reese!" as Mr. Walker nodded in agreement and continued, "Let me explain. As a small child we have no way of protecting ourselves. We are like sponges. We don't care if the water is dirty or the water is clean, we absorb it all. It makes no difference if it's positive or negative, good or bad, rich or poor, being accepted or being made fun of, included or rejected, built-up or putdown, loving or abusive. We absorb everything and initially have no way of protecting ourselves."

"It takes a responsible adult to provide protection in those early years. Some of us were fortunate and others less fortunate when it came to this protection and sometimes even under the best circumstances we are negatively impacted. By the age of four, our family has programmed us, along with our social and environmental surroundings, not to mention our genetic programming from past generations. We react to life's circumstances out of that programming," said Mr. Walker.

"Wow, then some people are screwed right from the start," added Reese.

Walker laughed and continued, "Well, not exactly. **It depends on where you put your focus.** Many people rise above negative experiences just fine and for some reason they only see the positive. But the majority of people have a different experience and learn to focus on the negative which, in turn, becomes their pattern in life and their reality.

"Imagine constantly hearing; you can't do that, you're not big enough, not strong enough, not pretty enough, too fat or too skinny, your feet are too big, you're dumb, you're stupid. Then you grow up thinking you're not going to be able to do anything right."

"That's a tough start to life," said Reese.

"Yes Reese, through constant reinforcement in our environment we are convinced or led to believe we are a certain way or we have to be a certain way," Mr. Walker continued, "Some kids are raised in an environment of positive reinforcement, but for many others, a large portion of their life experience is negative. Focusing on all the negativity attracts more of the same and too many people believe things can't change and perceive themselves as being stuck. Eventually they become angry, resentful, and hopeless. So I guess your earlier statement that they're screwed may hold true Reese."

"Wow, Mr. Walker," Reese blurted out, "Can you imagine being a fifth grader and having those thoughts and feelings? You see no future, no purpose, and no hope. You see no way out and then they expect you to do well in school? Gimme me a break! Now I see why we have problems in classrooms. While some kids want to learn, others are just there with all that garbage."

"Well Reese, maybe someday they'll understand the *Secret of the Can,*" said Mr. Walker.

Reese continued, "Wouldn't it be sad being told you'll never amount to anything as a kid and by 5th grade you believed it?"

"Not only is it sad but it happens often and in ways that are not always obvious," stated Mr. Walker as his voice softened, "But even sadder is the number of adults who have lived their entire life with that belief."

Whether you think you can or think you can't, you'll be right.

— *Henry Ford*

Mr. Walker noticed the time and quickly said, "We've covered a lot in class today. Let me try to summarize this before the bell rings. As a child we learn what we live, you become what you learn, and many people think of themselves through the words others use to define them. If the words are mostly critical, it sets up an inner conflict affecting our self-confidence. Inside we know we are good, but this is in conflict with what we are being told on the outside. If we are constantly told no, or we can't do it, or we're not good enough, then we begin to believe and behave as if we can't and we're not good enough. Those words become our beliefs and our beliefs become our reality and our reality is a direct result of every action we take or don't take. We become what others have told us we are," shared Mr. Walker.

"So rather than self-esteem many of us develop *other esteem*," Reese said with a new found excitement and understanding.

"Exactly!" answered Mr. Walker with a large smile and a nod of approval. "Many think there's something wrong with them; they think they're broken and they need fixed. The fact is – they're not broken. They were just given a false belief. So change your belief or your judgment about yourself and the world around you will change."

"Another important fact to remember is that to a child many things appear different than they do to an adult. I remember sledding in my backyard when I was around eight years old. As a kid I thought this was the biggest, baddest, meanest sledding hill around. When I went back to the house few years ago as an adult, I couldn't believe my eyes…it wasn't even a hill. How I had that perception as a child I'll never know. Shortly after we walked into the house and I walked up to the second floor into my old bedroom. The house that seemed like a big mansion when I was a child, all of a sudden was so small."

"We take many of our childhood perceptions and beliefs, especially our fears and self-doubts into our teenage and adult lives and it's those perceptions and beliefs that hold many back for a whole lifetime. But the good news is…that can all be changed."

Just then the bell rang. Reese sat on the far side of the room from the door and was usually the last student out, never rushed in his departure.

"Reese, how's basketball?" asked Walker.

"It's good Mr. W. You should stop by and watch practice tonight."

"I'll do that Reese," Walker stated.

January 28-After School Experience

Mr. Walker stopped by practice to watch Reese. Although you couldn't tell by looking at Reese's demeanor, he was quite the 3-point shooter, Mr. Walker thought to himself. To end practice at night he would shoot baskets until he made ten consecutive 3-point shots.

Reese was on fire tonight and after missing the first two he sunk the next 10.

Being there brought back memories for Austin as he thought to himself, there's nothing like hearing the snap of the net as the ball makes a big swoosh. After practice, Reese came immediately into the stands and sat next to Mr. Walker. "That's quite a shot you've got Reese!" Mr. Walker shared with enthusiasm.

"Wow, Mr. Walker! I didn't think you would actually show up," Reese shared with surprise! "Many people say things but don't follow through," Reese added.

"Maybe we should do a lesson on integrity and keeping our word in class tomorrow," Mr. Walker said jokingly.

"Mr. Walker, can you tell me *The Secret of the Can?*" asked Reese.

"Reese, let me share the beginning of the Secret with you. I believe everyone, either at birth or shortly after, receives a garbage can. As I shared in class today, we enter the world with generational family characteristics and patterns already in place whether they are positive or negative. That initially sets our behaviors in place and those behaviors are reinforced in our home environment as we grow. Then we go to school and we are supposed to have this thing they call self-esteem. But the self-esteem for many is replaced by *other esteem* where our self-concept is determined by the opinions, attitudes and words of others. And by now I'm sure you have discovered that words can blame, criticize, destroy and even kill… they usually don't kill physically, but *they kill the spirit and soul of those who absorb those words*. But it all goes back to *The Secret of The Can,*"

Mr. Walker explained and continued, **"With other esteem our behavior is based on what other people think. We have a tendency to act in ways that will cause others to like or accept us. Many times we will go against our own values."**

"But what's *The Secret of The Can* Mr. Walker?" asked Reese.

"Well, Reese we'd better be on our way home. I know you've got homework and I know Patches is wondering where his master is. See you in class tomorrow Reese." Walker said.

January 28 – Journal Entry

Mr. Walker came to my basketball practice tonight. It was like my father was there watching me. I can't really explain it. My whole life the only family that has ever seen me play is my mom and she rarely makes it. I asked him what *The Secret of The Can* was but I still don't know it. I have to find out.

Today's Life Skills class exit was much different than yesterday. Yesterday, almost dead silence, today, an energy and excitement among my classmates. They seemed excited about life. Free, uninhibited, and happy. There's something about Austin Walker and I don't know what it is. It's almost like he enters your mind and makes learning effortless. You learn but you don't realize it. It's like you've known him forever but yet you don't really know him. Like you're in a trance…Here we were in class and it was like Mr. Walker and I were the only two there. The rest of the world didn't exist. How can this be?

Chapter 3

Which Type of Person Are You?

"See things as you would have them be
...instead of as they are."
– Robert Collier

January 29 – Class Experience

Mr. Walker continued to share his wisdom with his Life Skills Class. Class interaction was showing him everyone was experiencing a change within himself or herself. Today Mr. Walker shared that he knew he only had a few precious years left on the planet. But throughout all his years, he discovered there are four types of people.

"The first type is a *victim*. As a small child, a *victim* begins to take things personally. If anything is going to go wrong, they are convinced it will happen to them. They began to develop what is called *'victim thinking'* or *'victim mentality.'* They focus on the problem, which keeps reinforcing the problem. This puts them into the feelings of self-pity and poor me. Continuing to tell the story focuses all their energy on their problems or the problems of others as they tell their tails of *if only, what went wrong, what could or may go wrong, illnesses, aches and pains.* All you have to do is listen to their words," shared Mr. Walker.

"Ya, my grandmother always has something wrong, Mr. W," said Mandi, "and she never has anything positive to say and she's always worried that something is going to go wrong. Last month she was complaining about her hand and this month it's her leg. She used to be fun, but anymore it's depressing to listen to her."

Sam added, "My dad is always focusing on the government and how things are so unfair. He thinks they're out to screw everybody."

Mr. Walker asked, "But what is it like being around him Sam?"

Sam looked down and talked softer, "Well, he's always angry or complaining. He's never happy."

"But is he a victim Sam?"

Sam thought for a minute figuring this was a Mr. Walker trick question then responded, "Mr. Walker, there's two answers to this. When you look at it he is not a victim but *his thinking makes him a victim.*"

"Great point Sam." smiled Walker, "Many times what makes a person a victim is their own thinking and if you listen to them they are always blaming someone or something else, but in reality they are the ones who are making themselves the victim."

"They begin to predict the future by only seeing things a specific way and miss many opportunities simply because they are convinced they can't. Keep in mind, this was a learned behavior early in life that they are unaware of. They seem to be trapped in a life of negative perception." Walker added.

"The good news is that all of this can be reversed! In a future class I will tell you how. But for now, think of your mind as a computer and your programming as the software. Some of the software was already installed at birth and other programs were added as a child. **If we want to change our outcomes in life we have to remove our old programming and add new."**

"So Mr. W," Sam called as he waved his hand, "With my dad, I find I'm beginning to think like him. How do I change that? I mean I love him and live in the same house, but yet I don't want to think and be like him."

"There are three steps we will cover in the coming weeks Sam. What we've covered over the past week is called **awareness and understanding.** In fact, how many of you are beginning to see things from a different point of view?" asked Mr. Walker. The entire class immediately raised their hands.

"Ya, my locker will never be the same!" joked Eric.

"The second step will be to learn about boundaries and not absorbing other people's trash and us not trashing others. Once we learn about the first two steps we will begin to reprogram ourselves by the use of goals and affirmations. Oh, and one more thing; we'll learn to see things differently. **The important thing for now, as we learn all of this, is that no matter where you are in life, it can be changed,**" Mr. Walker confidently shared.

"The second type is the victimizer. Victimizers use and abuse other people. They trash others, put others down, and make fun of people. They spread rumors and gossip and bully people, all at the expense of others. Many people victimize others without realizing it. They judge, make fun of and exclude others based on stereotypes, race, social-economic status, athletic ability, educational status and religious beliefs." Walker continued.

"**Victimizers and victims need each other to exist.** Victimizer's fish and victims take the bait. If a victimizer doesn't catch any fish they move to another pond. They can really wreak havoc in any environment. Now here's the problem – And Sam," Mr. Walker nodded to Sam, "this will answer your question about how *not* to be like your father."

"We each have a space around us. It's called our space or boundary and for our example let's say it looks like this:" Mr. Walker continued as he drew a figure on the Smartboard.

Walker went on as he listed, "Our boundary serves three purposes:"

1. It keeps me from going into the space of others.
2. It keeps others from coming in to my space.
3. It gives me the space to find out who I am.

"Look at your boundary as something that is flexible. It goes in or out – but it's always there.

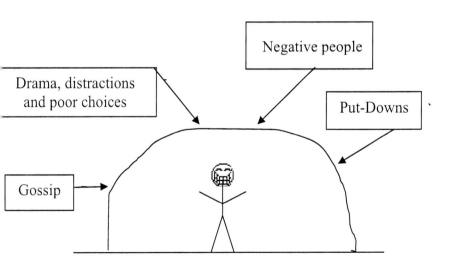

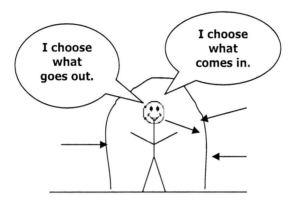

It's your filtering device. It's there to protect you, but it's **something you have to be aware that you possess."**

Sara raised her hand.

"Sara," Mr. Walker responded.

"Mr. Walker, so I'm going to walk around with this thing around me?" Sara said inquisitively.

"I can see we're getting much deeper into this today than I intended," Mr. Walker said sounding unsure about how the conversation would end up. "A few minutes ago, I said you would begin to **'see things differently,'** a boundary is something that is invisible, something you **create in your mind** as **a filtering system for all information that comes your way.** Remember, as a child we had no way to filter anything. We took the good with the bad. Now you are learning you have a choice…to pick and choose what comes into your space. In order to accomplish that, we are going to **visualize** a space around us so while we are learning this we have a point of reference in our mind. There are two types of boundaries; the emotional/intellectual boundary and the physical boundary."

"In fact, Sara will you and …ah...," said Walker as he scanned the room.

John raised his hand, "I will Mr. W!"

"…help me?" Mr. Walker finished. "Both of you come up to the front of the classroom. John, I want you to go over to my left, by the window and Sara I want you to go over by the door. Now, both of you face one another. This is a boundary exercise and you will be setting physical boundaries with each other."

"There are two rules for this exercise if it is going to be successful," said Mr. Walker as he looked seriously back and forth at each of them. "You must both be making eye contact with each other throughout the entire exercise and you must not laugh. Agreed?" Both of them acknowledged by nodding their heads. "Sara, I want you to walk toward John, while making eye contact and keep walking toward him until you feel uncomfortable. Then stop and adjust your distance between the both of you until you feel comfortable again. Any questions?" Both nod. "One more thing, members of the class it is your job to observe Sara and John's body language. – Okay, begin."

Sara slowly walks toward John and stops two feet away, then retreats backwards about a foot.

"Are you comfortable here Sara?" Mr. Walker asked.

"Yes, Mr. W."

"And you John?"

"Yep," said John trying to be macho.

Then Mr. Walker put the palm of his hand on Sara's back and lightly pushed her forward toward John until she began to stiffen up and resist until she was about two feet away. "Sara, are you comfortable?"

"No sir," Sara replied.

"How do you know?" Mr. Walker asked.

"I feel it inside," she replied.

Mr. Walker released his hand, thanked Sara and asked her to return across the room.

"Okay John, it's your turn." as Mr. Walker motioned. John walked toward Sara and stopped about a foot from Sara. Mr. Walker placed his hand between John's shoulders and lightly pushed him forward. There was obvious immediate resistance by John. "John are you comfortable?"

"No sss…sir," John replied.

"How do you know?"

"I'm not sure sir. I just know I'm not," said John.

"Very good John." Mr. Walker complimented.

"Class observations?" Mr. Walker asked.

"When you pushed them forward, the one standing still, seemed to sway backwards momentarily," shared Sam. "It was like you could see them enter into the other person's space. It was like a Star Trek thing, you know?"

"Very good observation Sam."

"Yah, Mr. W," said John, "That's exactly what it felt like! I could actually feel myself entering Sara's space and her entering mine."

"Sara would you agree?"

"Yes, Mr. Walker," she replied.

"You see, we each have this space or boundary around us, but we are unaware of it. We have learned to ignore it – not trust it. I am going to encourage each of you to start paying attention to this important tool. **Be aware of what you are feeling as you walk down the halls. Be aware of your space as well as the space of others**. It's part of our intuition or gut instinct and if you begin to pay attention to the feeling, you will develop it into a very useful tool. How many of you have been in a situation where it didn't feel right?" Everyone raises their hands. "How many of you have been in a situation where everything felt right and you knew, without a doubt, things would work out perfectly?" Again, all hands go up. "That's part of the same tool and I am going to encourage you to develop it. **But for now be aware that you each have your own Internal Guidance System**," Walker continued.

"One word of caution though," stated Mr. Walker. "It is a tool – and must be developed. You will need to learn how to use it. You will make mistakes along the way as you learn. But the more you use it and pay attention to it, the better you will become, the more you will trust it and the more you will make decisions from it. Highly successful people have mastered this and use it daily, especially in important decisions."

Walker explained, "The demonstration we saw today was about experiencing physical boundaries. The other type of boundary is the emotional/intellectual boundary. This one is a bit harder because it deals with words, attitudes and the way we judge and perceive different situations. You see, anyone can say anything they want to you, be as irresponsible as they want and you are the one who has to decide if it's true or not and what you're going to do with it. If someone says, 'You're an idiot,' now you have to decide if it's true or not. Your internal response might be, 'How did they know? It must be so obvious. Everybody probably knows.' But for that to happen you already have to think you're an idiot. Has anyone ever experienced those thoughts and the feelings connected to them?" A number of students insecurely raised their hands. "That was probably too personal of a question to ask in a classroom setting. I should have asked you to answer that question within yourself...my bad," apologized Mr. Walker.

"That's okay Mr. W," Delaney said, "That's what's so cool about this class. We are actually beginning to share who we really are and trust each other."

"Well thank you Delaney, but that was still irresponsible on my part," admitted Mr. Walker. "Now, where were we?"

Reese raised his hand.

"Yes, Reese," said Mr. Walker.

"You were saying if we believe someone else's negative comments about us is true, then we already have to believe it ourselves."

"Oh yes," stated Mr. Walker, "and if you hear it often enough you may even start thinking you're an idiot. Or you might say to yourself, 'I'm not an idiot. That idiot doesn't know what they are talking about,' and you continue on with your life not getting distracted. It's so important to know who you are and what you stand for. Because if you are not sure you will get caught up in endless questioning; is it true or not and become confused by all the irresponsible remarks people send your way. That third purpose of a boundary I shared with you in the beginning of class is very important – for it gives us the space to find out who we are. Once you know who you are, you are less likely to get sucked in by all the negativity in the world and you will be free to pursue your dreams and direction in life. Other observations? Yes Chad."

"John walked a lot closer to Sara than she did toward him," Chad commented.

"Why is that?" Mr. Walker asked.

Darryl responded, "Well, he's taller…bigger and he's a guy."

"And he really likes Sara and wishes she'd go out with him!" shouted Jason. Everyone laughed as both Sara and John turned a brilliant shade of red.

"So Chad, what you observed is that different people have different boundaries. Is that correct?" asked Walker.

"Yes sir," Chad replied, "But what if John would have kept walking and run right into her?"

"Ya like hugg'n and kiss'n all over her." joked Jason.

"You wish," Mandi taunted.

"Actually, all this leads to one last point," added Mr. Walker. "There are people with *"no boundaries."* People with no boundaries have no sense of being abusive, no sense of being abused, and have trouble saying no. **Victimizers are like this. They do not respect the space of others."**

Chad raised his hand.

"Yes Chad," as Mr. Walker acknowledged him.

"Victimizers … wouldn't they be what we call bullies?"

"Very good observation Chad and in many cases that is correct!" agreed Mr. Walker.

"Then people who get bullied would be victims," Chad added. So this stuff could actually help us eliminate problems in our school between students!"

"Precisely," Mr. Walker said with confidence as Chad reached out and gave Mr. Walker a high-five.

"When you walk down the hall between classes does everyone, for the most part, navigate through the crowd without running over other people?" asked Walker. The class shook their heads yes in response. "Well, that is an example of a boundary and how we respect each other's space. Have you ever walked down the hall and as you look up you realize the person walking toward you is going to run you over?" asked Mr. Walker.

"Yah, the football players do it all the time," said Jared, "They think they own the place."

"That's not true!" objected Mandi.

"That's cause you're a chick and they want something else from you," retorted Jared.

"Whatever," Mandi said, as if to make light of Jared's response.

"That's an example of a situation with someone who had no boundaries and someone who doesn't respect other people's boundaries. Those are difficult situations to say the least and we must decide how we are going to respond in each of those different situations," said Mr. Walker.

He continued, "People who are abusive in many cases have no sense that they are being abusive because no one ever told them no and meant it. When you set a boundary with this type of person, their immediate reaction is to challenge it or become angry. When that happens most people back down and change their mind. This becomes a pattern an abusive person becomes accustom to and becomes their normal behavior or habit. If you set a boundary and stick to it, initially you will get resistance, but if you stay strong during the resistance you will find on the other side will be respect. They will respect the boundary and more importantly they will respect you. But most importantly – you will respect yourself and when this happens it will ***turbo charge your self-esteem.***"

"On the other hand, people who get abused also have no boundaries because in getting abused you learn you do not have a right to your space. Again setting boundaries will be an important tool to acquire. When you set boundaries you will suddenly find no one is in your space and then who are you stuck with?"

"Yourself?" Sally stated as if asking a question.

"Very good Sally." responded Mr. Walker, "And imagine if you don't like yourself."

"Boy that would suck…big time!" said Eric.

Mr. Walker smiled and continued, "That is why most people don't set boundaries, it's easier to be in everybody else's business or let everybody in your business. Having boundaries means you have to take responsibility for yourself and many people are not ready to do that."

"See, if everybody is always in your space, you will never discover who you are. You will always be who others want you to be. You will find you are never good enough, you will never do it right, and if you had listened to them in the first place maybe your life would be better. You don't have to make decisions and you just follow along with the crowd."

"Would that be *other esteem*?" Reese asked.

"Yes Reese, that is one form of it."

Walker continued explaining, "If you're always in the space of others, you are constantly finding fault with them, judging and telling them what they did wrong. You are always keeping the spotlight on them so you never have to look at yourself."

"There are also people who have trouble saying no because they don't want to hurt other people's feelings and want everyone to like them. The problem is they never have time for themselves and they become over-committed and stressed. They become unhappy because in trying to please everyone else, they lose who they are. They become frustrated and angry with others and themselves although they rarely display it openly."

The bell rang – and no one got up to leave. It's like we were in a spell and for the first time in many of our lives Mr. Walker was connecting the dots…people and behaviors were beginning to make sense. Mr. W broke the trance by asking, "Didn't I hear a bell?" At that point, everyone snapped out of it and hustled to the door.

Reese, in his methodical departure, asked Mr. Walker, "What is the third type of person?"

Mr. Walker responded by saying, "That's not the question I thought you'd ask me. I thought you'd ask me to tell you *The Secret of the Can.*"

"I want to know that too!" said Reese with excitement.

"Which do you want to know more?" asked Mr. W.

"The Secret!" blurted out Reese.

Walker responded by saying, "The third type of person is a couch potato. See you tomorrow Reese and good luck in tonight's game."

January 29–After School Experience

Tonight was the Mustangs biggest challenge of the season. DePaul was undefeated and the Mustangs suffered their only loss two weeks ago. Walker went home and took care of Patches and decided to go to the game to support Reese. By the time Austin arrived it was the second quarter, standing room only and the Mustangs trailed by 3 points. Delaney and Sam saw Mr. Walker, Delaney ran over to him and gave him a hug and said, "Thank you!" Mr. Walker had become accustom to that experience over the years, as he had been instrumental in changing many lives.

Mr. Walker was standing along the wall on the north end of the court. With three minutes left in the game the Mustangs were down by 12 points. Reese dove to keep the ball from going out of bounds and in doing so landed right at Mr. Walker's feet. Mr. Walker reached down and gave Reese a helping hand up. The look of shock on Reese's face was priceless and turned into a big smile and a burst of energy. Reese went on to score 3 consecutive unanswered 3-point shots making the score 72 – 75. The Mustangs were down by 3 with less than a minute left.

The final score was 77 – 75 and even though the Mustang's lost, it was a great game.

January 29 – Journal Entry

Wow! What a game. I can't believe I'm writing tonight but I'm so wound up I have to do something. Normally I would be down after a loss but I know I played my best tonight. Seeing Mr. Walker really took me by surprise and it immediately shifted me into a feeling of great confidence. I've never felt that type of energy before. It was like I was totally in the zone, just the ball, the basket and me. Maybe that's what happens to ordinary people who do extraordinary things. I want to pay attention to that in the future.

Life Skills Class was interesting today. I learned a lot but the biggest thing was to treat everyone with respect regardless of his or her talent or ability. I see where it would be really easy for me to let basketball go to my head and think I'm better than everyone else. I hope that never happens. In class it seemed as if Mr. Walker was talking directly to me.

January 30 – Class Experience

The class energy level was a bit off today. The energy expended at the game last night combined with the loss left everyone a bit tired and it showed. Mr. Walker briefly reviewed the first two types of people, victims and victimizers. The third he shared is the couch potato. Everyone laughed and start to tease one another about fitting that role. It was a fun moment that created some energy in the room.

Mr. Walker shared, "Couch potatoes have great dreams and visions but they get distracted by the garbage of life, turn their backs on their dreams and direction, and their dreams become a faded part of the past. You see you can't go both directions at once. To go toward one is to turn your back on the other. **It's a matter of choice."**

"Mr. Walker?" John asked.

"Yes John."

"Last year, a friend of mine was at school every morning at 6 AM, in the weight room working out for football. He never missed a day. When it came around to football season he didn't go out for the team. He quit. Does that make him a couch potato?" John asked.

Mr. Walker did not answer but asked, "What did your friend make more important than football?"

"Well sir, over the summer he began to drink." John's eyes and voice dropped as he paused…"Sir, I'd rather not say. It's not right to talk about this in class."

"I agree John. Let me go back to your question about does that make him a couch potato?" continued Mr. Walker, "Your friend had dreams and direction and got distracted by the garbage of life and by definition he is a couch potato. But more than likely he will become a victim as he grows older, regretting his decision not to play football. I see countless people get distracted by the garbage of life giving up their dream for other things. The most important thing you can do is not let it happen to you, John."

"Thanks Mr. Walker. You can bet I won't let that happen to me." John replied confidently.

"One type of couch potato is like your friend. He was in action and then got distracted. But most **couch potatoes develop one or two specific habits. Procrastination** and…"

Doreen raised her hand. "Mr. W, what's procrastination?"

"Great question Doreen," he responded. "Have you ever put things off until the last minute?"

"I do that all the time," she admitted.

"Actually, Doreen **that is the number one problem people face and it's the behavior that holds them back.**" Walker explained.

"As an example," stated Mr. Walker, "let's say you have a school project due tomorrow. It's now 6 PM and you're in a panic because you have to go to the store to get supplies. Now your parents are included because all of a sudden they have to drop what they're doing and take you to the store. You're up late trying to get the project done and your parents are getting upset. The intensity builds and the next thing you hear is, 'How long have you had to do this project?' 'Why do you always wait till the last minute?' 'Next time you'll just have to take an 'F' because I'm not taking you to the store again!' So here's all this drama that was created."

Mr. Walker continued, "But all that really overshadows the real lesson here – Let's say your school project is a $20 job. To do it right you need to invest a specific amount of time and energy. But by doing the project the night before you are trying to do a $20 job with only $1 worth of time. That being said, your grade suffers but you get the project done. So you're wiping your forehead off, proud of yourself for pulling through at the last minute."

"Wow, Mr. Walker," Jason said, "You must have been at my house when I had to put my notebook together. I got a D on it, but at least I turned it in and passed."

"Was a D good enough?" asked Mr. Walker.

"No, not really, but it's better than an F," Jason justified.

"Jason, what grade would you have gotten on it had you not waited until the last minute?" asked Mr. Walker.

"Well sir, an A. It was an easy project."

"Jason, do you see how you are compromising yourself and selling yourself short? You could have easily gotten an A, but because of procrastination you were willing to accept the garbage of life and were relieved because you didn't get an F. Rather than focusing on the A, you focused on not getting an F and became a hero in your own mind because you didn't get an F," Walker stated.

"The other common habit is indecision. It's based on fear; fear of making a mistake, fear of making the wrong decision, fear of failure and sometimes fear of success. With both indecision and procrastination, putting things off builds stress and intensity. This adds more drama, which increases adrenaline. This develops energy and excitement in our life and we become addicted to the feeling. Then when things are boring we create drama and feel energized. The only thing it truly creates is negative results at our own expense and sometimes at the expense of others. This becomes a habit and a never-ending circle of intensity and insanity."

"Couch potatoes usually lack specific action toward specific goals. Eventually couch potatoes develop victim mentality and make their lack of progress and failures everybody else's fault. Have you ever known an adult where you thought to yourself, why didn't they do anything more with their life? They have all this knowledge and intelligence but they never did anything with their potential. They became comfortable on the couch and one day they began to think they were too old and that it's too late and they become victims of their own thinking," Walker said.

"Mr. W, you just described my mom," shouted Stephanie in amazement. "How can I help my mom Mr. W?"

"Stephanie, I believe you are beginning to see how behaviors and thinking patterns really dictate the outcomes you get in life. The first thing you must do is put into action what you are learning in class, for yourself. Soon after that you will know the HOW," shared Mr. Walker. "Remember, **regardless of where you are in life, your habits and behaviors can all be reversed.** But that is something for a later class." Mr. Walker paused and continued, "Again, I share this information with you only for awareness and understanding."

"The fourth type of person is the **Keeper of the Keys.** Keepers have purpose, Keepers have passion, rarely do they get distracted and they never give up. For somewhere along the journey of life Keepers have either been given or discovered *The Secret of the Can"*…and at that moment the bell rang.

February 3 – Journal Entry

Life Skills has a new vibe this week. None of us cut each other any slack. Jake started to make fun of Sam and his girlfriend breaking up and everyone jumped on Jake saying, "victimizer!" Delaney was stressed about a report she had due tomorrow plus all her other homework and Mandi said, "Sounds like a cross between a victim and a procrastinator." Jake added, "No I bet she was a couch potato."

I find myself labeling people in my mind over the past few days. I am beginning to see people when they are playing or being a victim…it's so obvious now. I used to feel sorry for them, now I just say a prayer for them or send a positive thought to them, because standing up for yourself is so easy. All it takes is a decision to do it and practice. Victimizers…well, it's amazing how we put up with their stuff.

I've noticed the largest group of people is the couch potatoes. It seems like everybody wants to be successful but they expect success to come to them. *Maybe we have to go to success.* Does success even know I exist? Does success know my name? Does success even care? I guess I really shouldn't waste time thinking about this because I really want to be a "Keeper of the Keys" and **I can see how Mr. Walker is giving us the skills to all be Keepers.**

A couple of kids had a meltdown on each other in the hall today. Mr. Walker broke it up and took a punch in the process. Regardless of what happens, Mr. Walker always remains calm and takes things in stride.

Chapter 4

The Secret of the Can

"If you judge people,
…you have no time to love them."
-- Mother Teresa

February 5 – Classroom Experience

Three girls got called down to the office out of Mr. Walker's class today. I'm not sure what's going on but rumors are that it has to do with a party three weeks ago. How cool is that! Everyone has some drama to focus on for a few days – so gossip will be flyin. This should be good!

February 5–After School Experience

Reese approached Mr. Walker after class. "Mr. Walker, I've been watching you and you never take offense to rude comments from students. You always address negative situations between students and you are never rude to anyone. Yesterday you got hit breaking up a fight, yet today you were smiling and talking with each of them. No matter what the situation, you're always calm and focused. How can you do that?"

"Reese, let me ask you this: ***How do you think I do it?***" Walker asked.

Reese looked up and thought for a moment, then looked down, smiled and said, "You know *The Secret of the Can*, Mr. Walker."

A big smile came from Mr. Walker as he said, "Very good Reese! I notice you and your friends are having a lot of fun in class and learning to identify victim, victimizer and couch potato behaviors in each other. You guys bust each other left and right every day and that is a good way to create awareness of our regular behaviors. Once you've created the awareness you must move past your old behaviors and when you know *The Secret of the Can* and apply it, the garbage of life no longer distracts you. Then you will become a Keeper of the Keys. Remember, **Keepers have purpose and passion, rarely do they get distracted and they never give up.**"

"So Mr. Walker, you're teaching us how to be Keepers and you are showing us what Keepers look like on the outside," Reese stated in a questioning yet confident voice.

"Reese, your perception amazes me," shared Mr. Walker. "I know people three and four times your age who still don't get it."

"Mr. Walker, can I ask a question?" asked Reese. Mr. Walker nodded. "Math teacher, Mr. Birda, is he a Keeper?"

"Yes indeed," Walker replied.

"And Miss Hill, Mr. T and Coach Paul?" asked Reese.

"Indeed they are." replied Mr. Walker.

Reese stared at the floor and Mr. Walker observed a tone of sadness start to overtake Reese's body. "Reese, where did you just go in your mind?"

"Well sir, I just realized there are only four teachers...well five including you, who are Keepers of the Keys in this whole school and then there's my mom who has spent her whole life as a victim. Sure, she's worked hard to provide for us but her thinking is that of a victim so she's never known true happiness," explained Reese.

"Yes, Reese I understand your sadness, but I also see something very special in you. I met your mother last week and she shared how I seemed to be the father figure you were missing in your life and how grateful she was for that. She told me she has really never told you about your father other than he was kind, giving and loved by all and that you were born with a purpose in this world. I asked her if I could share his story with you and she agreed."

Walker continued, "Reese, your first father was diagnosed with bone cancer when he was 23 years old, shortly after he and your mom were married. The cancer was spreading rapidly. Your grandparents pulled all their money together to find him the best medical doctors available, which was in New York City at the time. They amputated his right arm and shoulder hoping to stop the cancer. During this time your mom and dad didn't make love... because in his words, 'He didn't want to leave her with a burden.' But on St. Patrick's Day, he had a change of heart and they made love one time in one year. Now, what are the odds of you being here...a million to one? Regardless, you are not an accident but an 'on purpose'. Their intention was to create a child and they did."

"She also shared with me that you had an older sister. She was stillborn at birth. Your mom went through a lot in a short two-year period of time. She fell in love, got married, buried a daughter, buried a husband, and had a son. Reese, you were born out of pure love. As your mom has told you, you are here for a special reason and when I heard your mom's story, I immediately realized why you and I have met."

Tears rolled down Reese's cheeks as he reached out and hugged Mr. Walker. The hug was as if it had been waiting 17 years to be given. It was an embrace Austin would never forget. Mr. Walker broke the silence as he said, "You, my son, are ready to learn *The Secret of the Can.*"

It was now three hours since school ended. The sun had set and there was noise outside as Mr. Haines, the janitor, arrived at the door to clean the classroom. Reese looked at Mr. Haines and then at Mr. Walker. Reese smiled and whispered, "**There's another Keeper.** That's' six!" Mr. Walker smiled and nodded in agreement.

"Reese, are you hungry?" Mr. Walker asked.

"Starving." said Reese.

"Let's go and I'll buy dinner and share with you *The Secret of the Can!*"

"Yes!" shouted Reese.

"Call your mom so she knows where you're at," added Austin.

"Oops. Good idea," said Reese.

They stopped at a small Mexican restaurant in town, placed their orders with the waiter and immediately dug into the salsa and chips. Reese realized he was angry and felt cheated because his father died before he was born. "Wow, Mr. Walker," Reese began, "I never knew how much my dad loved me until today. And my mom…I had no idea she dealt with all that. All these years I've painted myself as a victim when I was actually a victor and someone who *was given* the greatest gift of love and life."

"Yes Reese," Mr. Walker continued, "**There are many things that have happened in the lives of others that we never know about, yet we judge them.** I think *The Secret of the Can* will help you though."

Mr. Walker began, "The first part of the secret is: *Everyone has a garbage can.*"

Reese looked at Mr. Walker with a puzzled expression on his face.

Mr. Walker continued, "Let me explain. Keep in mind, understanding and awareness is the first step. I believe everyone was born with or shortly after birth received a garbage can. We don't use it to get rid of negativity; but instead we use it to hold on to negativity and carry it around with us."

After a long pause, Mr. Walker continued speaking each word slow and deliberate,

"The real secret is…The can doesn't come with a lid."

"Finding the lid will be the most life-changing event anyone can experience for it will truly change your life."

"Reese, do you know all the things we have covered in class; having no protection as a child, absorbing everything, all those genetic, environmental, economic and social factors? **None of those mean anything once you find the lid,**" Walker explained.

"So all you taught us is meaningless?" Reese asked.

"Everything I have taught you serves a purpose. Without it we would never have taken the **first step**, which **is awareness and understanding of what is happening around us and how we continue to create the same circumstances and situations. Many people try to skip this vital and important step and then wonder why they continue to get the same results. They have dreams and set goals but continue to get distracted by the garbage of life.** Many adults have gone through life struggling because they have designed their world to limit themselves. **Once you find the lid, the garbage of life will no longer distract you.** You will have the freedom to pursue your dreams and direction in life. But many people never get this. They never discover the secret."

"How would understanding this as a teenager help you? What would that mean for your future Reese?" Mr. W. asked.

"Well, **I wouldn't be limited or held back,**" said Reese.

"Exactly," said Mr. Walker. "You could freely pursue your dreams."

"Let's continue on with awareness and understanding. There are three ways we fill up our can. The first is by trashing others; quite common in the school setting, wouldn't you agree? It happens when we try to rise above or be better than others or it can happen when our can gets full from being dumped on and, in turn, we empty it on to others. You know, putting people down, making fun of someone, spreading rumors or gossip, calling someone names or making fun of their body size, shape, or looks. It's frustrating for me to see kids who have a lot of talent use their position to tear others down that aren't as gifted as them. It's such a loss because here they are with the opportunity to pull someone up and actually take their own game to a higher level."

"That's what victimizers do isn't it?" Reese asked.

"You're learning quickly," Mr. Walker said with excitement.

"Trashing others is the easiest one to change, but at the same time, the hardest because it calls for us to close our mouths. If you're used to hearing criticism and being told how you can't do anything, you're always wrong or you'll never amount to anything…you won't have a vocabulary for positive support. It becomes very hard to say positive things about others if you haven't heard them yourself. When it comes to complimenting or saying good things about others we are speechless, we don't have the vocabulary or know the language for speaking positively and supporting one another. I remember years ago I showed a thirty-minute 'Simpson's' TV program in the classroom. I removed all the advertisements, so the whole episode was only eighteen minutes long. I wanted everyone to realize how easily TV teaches us to put each other down. The assignment was to count the number of times Bart was put down or made fun of in a shaming or degrading way."

"So how many, Mr. W?" Reese impatiently asked.

"Thirty-eight times in eighteen minutes of TV. We easily learn to "dis" or trash others by making fun of them and putting them down and the reward is people laugh and think we are funny all at someone else's expense. We have been programmed to focus on the negative and not see the goodness in others. We have been programmed to see their flaws and imperfections and then shine a spotlight on them for others to see. Most people trash others unconsciously. In other words, they are **unaware** that their words are putting others down or they are making fun of someone."

Reese asked, "What is the difference between having fun with someone and trashing someone?"

"Reese, I ask myself the question: Am I having fun at the expense of someone else?"

"But Mr. Walker, what about when you're with friends and joking around and stuff?" asked Reese.

"First, with a lid, you don't take anything personally. With your friends your mindset is that of fun so your lid is already in place as your filtering device. But what is really great is that when you **start playing big, say at the Major League level of life, you and your friends become so supportive of each other that making fun of each other rarely happens. You're too busy enjoying the greatness and success of life to get distracted by those old behaviors.**"

Walker continued, "Not trashing others is especially important for victimizers to master. As long as they continue to trash others the garbage of life will distract them."

"So the behavior of trashing others is holding them back?" asked Reese.

"Precisely Reese." added Mr. Walker, "Changing this takes awareness and then conscious practice. Closing your mouth is a hard thing to do and in the beginning you always have the option to say I'm sorry."

"The second way we fill up our can is by absorbing trash from others," Walker added.

"Let me guess," Reese said. "These are the victims."

Mr. Walker continued, "**When they change their victim behavior they become a completely different person, a person of true power.** Many people are made fun of, teased, put down or criticized and they develop victim-like behaviors. As this behavior continues, those who absorb all this negativity become resentful and angry inside. They keep all that emotion inside and it leads to depression, negative self-talk, lack of self-confidence and they see themselves as a victim. Occasionally, they will see the only way out is suicide or violence. Graffiti, destruction of property, lack of respect and school shootings are some of the ways this can be played out. It shows up as uncontrolled or misdirected anger or an attitude of indifference."

"Finding the lid is where anyone who is a victim can **immediately begin to change** his or her life. Victims are masters of absorbing trash from others and they develop the habit of seeing themselves as a victim in most situations. That's part of the *victim mentality or victim thinking*. Finding the lid will keep you focused on your dreams and direction. Imagine someone putting you down or making fun of you and you not taking it personally or reacting. You could smile and continue on, no longer distracted by the garbage of life and the best part is you will move faster, freer and easier toward your dreams and direction in life."

"I might add here, when you are distracted by the garbage of life you miss so many opportunities because your back is turned away from your dreams and you can't see that which you are not facing."

"Our own negative self-talk is the third way we absorb garbage – we trash ourselves. We put ourselves down. We say we are sorry and apologize when we didn't do anything wrong. We find ourselves rationalizing for just being who we are and not being perfect. This tends to be not as obvious, as it has become woven into our society and many cultures. It gets reinforced in our music, TV, videos, video games, in school, the workplace and in the family. The constant reinforcement makes change difficult. Take your classmates Reese, many of them are learning skills in class to create change in their lives, but only three or four of you will continue to use and develop those skills past the end of the school year. Those who continue to use the skills will soon be **Keepers of the Keys** and as a result, create a successful life way beyond their wildest dreams. They will know and use **The Three Keys of Success,**" stated Walker.

Reese asked, "Mr. Walker, which do you eliminate first?"

Mr. Walker replied, "You have already taken the biggest step. I can't stress enough that with awareness and understanding you are over halfway there. That in itself will change a lot."

"From now on you will find yourself in situations where you can begin to **use your lid**. By closing your mouth in the middle of putting someone down, you've just used your lid. By not absorbing or taking a negative comment or putdown from another person personally, you've just used your lid. Thinking positive thoughts about yourself and encouraging yourself, you've just used your lid! From then it's just a matter of time as you change habits by putting specific behaviors in your life and that Reese – **will make your success inevitable**."

"Remember, all this takes time…practice…and reinforcement," Walker added.

"So all this happens within you and everyone can do this if they choose to?" Reese asked.

"Yes. The easiest way is to see yourself doing it."

"What do you mean?" asked Reese.

"Let me ask you this. When you are shooting three-point shots after practice, do you see yourself making those?"

"Well, yes sir." Reese said confidently.

"As you sit here, can you see yourself in your mind, making a three-point shot?"

"That's easy Mr. W! It's a swish every time."

"That's called visualization. **When you visualize something it makes it happen that much faster and that much easier.** Top athletes use it all the time to become top performers. But I'm going to encourage you to use it in every part of life Reese!" Mr. Walker expressed. "See yourself passing that test, see yourself turning in your homework, see yourself being helpful to others and see yourself using your lid."

"Wow," said Reese, "I was thinking the secret was this big profound thing and it's so simple, yet no one sees it."

Mr. Walker added, "Sadly enough Reese, there are a great deal of people who go through life and were never shown or discovered the secret. I'd like to change that. How about you?"

"Do you think it's possible Mr. Walker?" asked Reese.

"For **Keepers of the Keys** anything is possible. Keepers have purpose and passion, rarely do they get distracted and…"

Reese jumped in and shouted, "They never give up!"

At that moment Reese put his hand up and gave Mr. Walker a high-five.

"Well," Mr. Walker said as he looked around the restaurant, "When we got here the place was filled. Now the place is empty and I don't remember seeing anyone leave. Show me where you live Reese and I'll drop you off at home."

Walker dropped Reese off and realized it was 11 p.m. He and Reese had been talking for over 8 hours. Mr. Walker smiled knowing his purpose was almost fulfilled. He hurried home realizing he had forgotten all about Patches. When Mr. Walker arrived home there was Patches in all his excitement, tail wagging and barking with joy. "I bet you're glad to see me boy."

Mr. Walker, as was his custom, sat in his chair with Patches and reflected on his day and prayed, "Dear Lord, thank you for this day and all the goodness it has given me. I am so happy and grateful to have found Reese and I realize my work here is almost done. Please continue to grant and give me guidance and work through me in everything I do to help others. Amen."

Meanwhile, as Reese walked into his house, he felt tears come to his eyes as he was immediately filled with the same feelings he experienced hours earlier when he learned about his father and the sacrifices his mother had made. Reese went over to his mother while fighting back his tears and gave her a big hug and said, "Mom, I love you. Thank you." Reese continued upstairs to his bedroom as Ms. William's became overwhelmed with emotion. It was as if the past 17 lonely years of raising Reese alone were now lifted.

February 5 – Journal Entry

I am torn right now but at the same time what an awesome day. I guess I need to start where I'm at right now. I've been angry for many years feeling cheated in life because I didn't have a father and here I find out that my being born was the greatest gift ever. I can't believe how understanding what my mom went through changes all my anger to gratitude. **I wonder if a lot of the trouble in the world is just that – lack of understanding.** Even though I never heard my dad say he loved me, I now know he truly did and my mom carried both of their love. I don't know if these tears are happiness or sorrow. I just know they are…guess it doesn't matter.

Along with everything today I finally learned *The Secret of the Can*. Wow, how simple…everyone has a can…but it doesn't come with a lid. Life will never be the same from now on. This will be a day just as important as my birthday and I will celebrate it every year from now on…February 5th. It's almost like I am born again, but not really. How about I call it the day success became inevitable or inevitable success day. This is the day I officially started my "Journey of Success." Today, February 5, is the day I, Reese Williams, take responsibility for my life. I will eliminate judgment of others by listening and understanding them. I will take action steps each day toward my goals. I like that! Be awesome in your game tomorrow night! Reese, goodnight and I love you.

PS. Mr. Walker is like a father to me. In one night I go from feeling cheated that I never had a father to feeling like I have two of the best father's in the world...go figure.

"When I am anxious it is because I am living in the future. When I am depressed I am living in the past."

– Anon.

Chapter 5

Letting Go

"Your past is always going to be the way it was. Stop trying to change it."

--Anon.

Over the next few months Mr. Walker shared a vast amount of information and lessons including the *Three Keys of Success* with Reese. Looking at Reese you could see that he had changed. There was something about him that permeated everyone and everything around him, similar to that of Mr. Walker's presence.

February 7 – Journal Entry

We ended our basketball season last night with another victory, which gave us 19 wins and 3 losses for the season. In the past I would have focused on our three losses and probably would have kept asking myself "what if" I would have made this shot or "what if" we would have just played a bit harder in the first quarter. I'm already thinking about next season now and using the First Key of Success has really allowed me to see things differently.

I've been so focused on basketball that I haven't spent much time with my friends. I think I'm going to make it a point to spend some time with them. No more practice after school everyday. But now that I think about it track season is just around the corner and before you know it I'll be practicing everyday again. I'd better make time for my friends right now. I'll call Delaney and Sam tomorrow.

We got a new kid in class today. I don't even remember his name. That's sad. I think he was living with his dad and had to move in with his mom. That must suck to have to change schools like that. Of course maybe it was for the better. I'm not sure I could handle something like that. That would have really messed up my basketball. I would have been one angry dude and had more than a chip on my shoulder. I think I'll make it a point to talk to him next week. Yeah, that's a great idea Reese. By talking with him you could listen and then you would understand him better and you wouldn't judge him.

You were really awesome this year in basketball. Sleep well tonight and call Delaney and Sam tomorrow. Peace dude and don't forget – YOU ROCK!

February 8 – Journal Entry

Today I caught up with Delaney and Sam and we spent most of the day together. It felt great to just sit around at Delaney's and do almost nothing. I can't believe we spent most of the time talking about things we've learned in Mr. Walker's class. We each took a turn and shared one of our big goals in life. Delaney wants to be a journalist who writes major magazine articles for the Arts and theatrical reviews for Broadway plays. She also wants to write a play for teens that shares an important message about success.

Sam gets straight A's. He was originally thinking of going to our local community college because he really didn't believe in himself. But with everything he's learned in Life Skills class, he says he's thinking much bigger and would like to go to a bigger university and get a degree in business marketing. What is it that causes people not to believe in themselves? Here is Sam, a straight A student who didn't believe in himself. Come on Sam…go figure.

As for myself, my goal is to make a positive difference in my school. I'm not sure how that will happen, but Mr. Walker says we don't have to know the how right now…we just have to know the what. We ended our day all agreeing to become Keepers of the Keys and support each other through life regardless of where our journeys take us. That was a great feeling!

February 10 – Journal

I took a risk today and ate lunch with the "new kid in class." Actually, his name is Jared. He's quiet, but once you get him talking I found he is quite funny and has a great sense of humor. He had to move in with his mom because his dad went to prison. His mom is an alcoholic and cocaine addict who has been clean and sober now for five years. He's really proud of her. You could tell it in his voice and how his face lit up when he talked about her. One of the things Jared said was, "I'll never be like my parents." I immediately thought of all the things we had already learned from Mr. Walker and how Jared could use that information right now in his life.

I have to ask myself, how can I take what we've learned in Mr. Walker's class and share it with others? After all, Mr. Walker won't be our teacher much longer and I'm not sure if anyone will ever teach us this stuff. Knowing this info could make the difference in Jared's life.

The three girls that got called out of class returned today. Wow! Sixteen girls were suspended. That has to be a record. Each got five days OSS. All were at Stephanie's 18th birthday party and her parents rented a party van. What were they thinking…or maybe they weren't. Everything was cool for a month but pictures with alcohol and some other things made it to the internet and since all the girls were involved in sports they got busted and suspended. So much for this year's swim team. Even though the girls are back in class, the trouble is just starting for Stephanie's parents.

February 26 – Journal Entry

We learned about the brain today in Life Skills class. My mind is really working overtime on this and I can see how this will help me in track and basketball. Oh yes, and in school. I can't believe they don't teach this stuff to us all throughout school. The subconscious mind goes 24/7 regardless of who you are and you can make it work for you by pointing it in a specific direction just before you go to sleep at night. If I go to bed dreaming about my goals, my subconscious mind will find ways to achieve them, all while I'm sleeping. Successful people use this method all the time. But if I watch the news and then go to bed, all that garbage is running around in my brain all night or if I have a fight or argument and go to bed angry, then all that stuff is running around in my mind. Mr. Walker says, "Always end your day with a success and if you've had a bad day then read a page out of a book, review something from school, or just spend a few minutes praying or thinking of things in life you are grateful for. All of these are successes."

Another thing we learned today was that if I review my notes from the day's classes, just before I go to bed at night, it makes studying easier. The short-term memory information (the notes I just reviewed) gets transferred into the long-term memory between the 6th and 8th hour of sleep. Now there are two problems with this approach. First, I have to take notes in class so I have them to read before I go to bed. The second, I have to get 8 hours of sleep so the information gets transferred. I'm not sure which is the easier of the two.

March 1 – Journal Entry

Sunday night and I'm down. I don't know why Sunday nights are like this. I just feel really lonely inside. Last week we learned – **a child needs only one trusted adult in their life to be successful.** I realized today Mr. Walker is that one trusted adult in my life. Couldn't have been anyone better.

March 4 – Journal Entry

I had a dream last night. I was using my garbage can lid as a shield but it kept me stuck by the garbage can and I couldn't get away. I was frustrated and freaking out when Mr. Walker appeared. "Reese," he said, "You are ready for the final lesson, which has two parts. First, many hold on to the pain and anger of the past, all the hurt, sorrow, sadness, and resentment. Doing so keeps you a victim of your past. **The past will only have as much power as you give it and once you have learned to let go, you may still have the memory, but the feelings will change to feelings of forgiveness, appreciation, love, and compassion. Pray for others – then release them.**"

"Second, as you are now experiencing, we get very good using the lid as a shield. We block out negativity, we stop judging others and putting people down. We also begin to eliminate negative self-talk and reduce our negative thinking patterns, but at times you will still be surrounded by negativity. Remember Reese; if you want to be a Keeper of the Keys you must never give up.

Now Reese, take the final step, place the lid on the can and let it go. This is the final action to total freedom. Letting go gives you the total freedom to pursue your dreams and direction with passion and energy. And at that moment you will know you are the Keeper of the Keys".

March 19 – Journal Entry

I am starting to see how easily racism, prejudice and stereotyping keeps people stuck as victims and victimizers. Once you start to focus on any of these as an issue, the garbage of life immediately distracts you. Anger, blame, poor me and self-pity become your reality. All of this creates a lot of drama. It seems that many people are born into situations like this. Is it passed from generation to generation? How do people break the cycle? Duh, Reese...use "The Secret of the Can." Wow, that would be hard to become a Keeper of the Keys, but if you do, you will have the opportunity to really make a difference in the world.

April 17 – Journal Entry

Track season is in full swing. Our Life Skills lessons on **visualization** have helped me be one of our top competitors. Thanks to Mr. W!

Tomorrow will be a special day for me. It's the anniversary of my dad's death. I never knew the date before. I was too angry to really care. Now it's important, as I know my dad is always with me. Remembering the day is my own special way of thanking him. I also find it interesting that tomorrow is Mr. Walker's last day in our classroom. Mrs. Kliner and her newborn baby, Allison, are doing very good and she will be back in the classroom after Spring break to end the school year. The past few months have flown by. Everyone looks forward to Mr. Walker's daily lessons in Life Skills. But it still seems like he's talking directly to me. Some days I wonder if this is real.

I talk to my mom more now than ever. Yesterday I shared with her about my loneliness on Sunday nights. She began to tell me the story of the night after my dad's funeral. There had been people around to support her through my dad's illness and funeral and the first time she was completely alone was a Sunday night and since she was pregnant with me at the time and it was such an emotional experience, she said I may have had the same experience.

April 18 – Class Experience

We spent our whole class on gratitude and appreciation. We met in the large carpeted meeting room just outside the Auditorium. All the tables and chairs were removed. We had to choose a partner and tell them everything we appreciated about them and then they would do the same for us. Then we had to find someone else. How does Mr. Walker pull this stuff off! It seemed like a dream.

The last person Reese ended up with was Mr. Walker. Reese started first. He could feel emotion welling up in his throat and all he could get out were eight words…

"Thank you for introducing me to my dad," he said holding back his emotions and gave Mr. Walker a big hug.

Holding back his own tears, Mr. Walker began, "Reese, when we first met you were very angry – your father died before you were born and you felt slighted. It was unfair. Other kids had a father even if divorced. You weren't aloud to play football because your mom didn't want you to get hurt. She was overprotective and you resented her for that and you resented your father dying and leaving you all alone. But today Reese, I see someone who appreciates their father's act of love shortly before he died. I see someone who is grateful for the gift of life he has been given. I see someone who has forgiven and truly let go of the past. I appreciate you for taking responsibility for the reason this has all come to pass. Reese, **you are the Keeper of the Keys!**"

Walker gave Reese a big hug and at that moment the bell rang. Everyone gave each other high-fives as they left down the hall. You could see the pride Reese possessed beaming throughout his entire body.

Reese looked back and said, "Mr. W. I've got to go – we have a track meet today. I'm running the 400 m for the first time." Reese bent down as if he were starting the race and jumped toward the door.

Mr. Walker called to him, "Reese." Mr. W threw him the pouch he carried on his belt and shouted, "Good luck Reese."

Chapter 6

Commitment

*"When you know what you want
and you want it badly enough,
you will find the ways to get it."*
– Jim Rohn

December 12 – After School

It's Friday night and the Mustang's are up against their rival, the Eagles, who are also undefeated. As a senior, Reese is starting guard and has already received player of the week twice for his performance on and off the court.

Reese has applied the lessons he has learned from Mr. Walker in all aspects of life. Tonight's game is the toughest challenge yet, but in true form; Reese is on fire from what Mr. Walker used to call the "Land of Three". That's where you practice big, show up big and make it big. The Mustang's easily beat the Eagles 86 – 51. Reese was eight for ten from the "Land of Three" and ended the game with 31 points, a new school record for three pointers and personal scoring! After the game Reese sat in the locker room in a moment of prayer, expressing gratitude for his talent and wondering if he'll ever see Mr. Walker again. Puzzled…Reese thought to himself…here I am, the hero of the game, my best game ever and I'm thinking of Mr. Walker.

As Reese left he remained within himself and walked through the now almost empty gym. He looked up in the stands where Mr. Walker used to sit and watch him practice. Reese saw an old man walking down from the stands. He immediately thought of Mr. Walker.

He stopped and stared for a moment and started to say, "Mrrrr…"

The old man said, "That's a wicked three-point shot you've got boy, almost impossible to defend. Mr. Walker told me about that shot."

Reese shouted out with excitement, "Mr. Walker!"
The old man put his arm on Reese's shoulder and they walked over to the bleachers and sat down. The old man looked down at the ground and then into Reese's eyes.

"Reese, Mr. Walker came back in the classroom last year for one reason. He hadn't found the perfect student yet. He needed to share *The Secret of the Can* with someone who could **share the secret with others.** He knew his time was limited here and toward the end he was concerned he may not find the perfect student. You, Reese, were the perfect student, Mr. Walker's best student. I know you've been wondering what happened to him and he asked me to tell you after tonight's game. He said in doing so you would know he is here with you."

"Reese, Mr. Walker passed away last May." There was a long pause before Mr. Jamison continued, "And somehow he knew that tonight would be your best game ever. You broke two school records and convincingly beat a team of equal talent."

Tears slowly rolled down Reese's checks and although he was filled with sadness you could see a small smile on his face, as Reese knew deep inside...Mr. Walker had never left...and it was the same as with his father.

The old man continued, "Reese, before he passed away, I made three commitments to him. He asked I do three things:"

1. Talk to you after the game tonight.
2. Let you know you truly know *The Secret of the Can.*
3. Share with you that it is your responsibility to **share the secret with others.**

"Reese, keeping our commitments, no matter how difficult, shows our integrity and self-esteem. To be a Keeper of the Keys you **must** keep your commitments; commitments to *others* and most importantly ...commitments to *yourself*."

Reese left the gym that evening the big star. While everyone was celebrating, Reese took the opportunity to think about and appreciate how his life had changed over the past year.

December 13 – Saturday Morning

Reese brought his clothes down to the laundry room. This was one of those normal routines that make life easier at home. Although Reese's mom tried to get him to do this for years, it was Mr. Walker's class that got Reese to realize the importance of being organized. When Reese appeared in the laundry room his mom was in the midst of transferring the clothes from the washer to the dryer. Reese could hardly contain himself and began telling his mother about the old man, Mr. Jamison, the night before. Just as Reese shared that Mr. Walker had passed away, she noticed a leather pouch on the windowsill.

"Reese, do you know who this belongs to?" she asked.

"Wow Mom! Where'd you find that?"

"It was in the laundry last spring and I keep forgetting to ask you about it," she said apologetically.

Again, Reese felt his insides well up with emotion as tears came to his eyes as the memory of all the experiences he had with Mr. Walker came back. "Mr. Walker gave it to me our last day of class," Reese said as he grabbed the pouch and ran toward his room. Then he briefly stopped in the doorway, turned around and ran back to his mom. He smiled, gave her a hug and said I love you. Then was off and running back toward his room. Reese sat on the edge of his bed hesitating not knowing what he would find inside the pouch. A thought came from within; Keepers trust and take action and Reese quickly opened the pouch. In it were three keys and a handwritten letter.

Reese,

Congratulations on your game! I know if you are reading this that you have spoken with my old friend, Mr. Jamison, and he shared with you my requests. As a "Keeper of the Keys" I know I could count on him. Keepers are the essence of responsibility and commitment.

There were times when I was worried and concerned that I would leave this world before I found the perfect student to share the secret with and pass on the Keys. Sometimes, even I, have moments of distrust — it is so easy to slip into thoughts of worry and fear; it's part of being human. But as a "Keeper of the Keys" it is not okay to stay there! Remember, everything always works out if you trust and take action.

Also remember how you came into this world. What were the odds? You and I both know you were born with a special reason and until now that reason was unclear. Each person, regardless of who they are, has a special reason for being here!

(2)

But as you have learned, most people get distracted by the garbage of life and never find their purpose.

Reese — you truly know "The Secret of the Can" and through you, the students in your school will have such an advantage, but don't stop there! It is your responsibility as a "Keeper of the Keys", to share this with your peers and youth around the world.

You do not have to know how you will do it at this time. The how will come later. All you have to know is in your pouch are the "Three Keys of Success" and you are now the "Keeper of the Keys." Using these keys will give you everything you need...

... trust and take action.

And now you know you _can_!

With Love and Gratitude,

Mr. W.

To discover how Reese rose to the
challenge log on to
www.thesecretofthecan.com/reese

"The Secret of the Can is the starting point,
the foundation on which you build your life
of success."